Threads of Thoughts

Threads of Thoughts
- Ronok Ghosal

 BLACK EAGLE BOOKS

USA address:
7464 Wisdom Lane
Dublin, OH 43016

India address:
E/312, Trident Galaxy, Kalinga Nagar,
Bhubaneswar-751003, Odisha, India

E-mail: info@blackeaglebooks.org
Website: www.blackeaglebooks.org

First International Edition Published by
BLACK EAGLE BOOKS, 2024

THREADS OF THOUGHTS
by **Ronok Ghosal**

Copyright © **Ronok Ghosal**

Cover & Interior Design: Ezy's Publication

ISBN- 978-1-64560-565-2 (Paperback)

Printed in the United States of America

Preface

Welcome to my poem collection, a journey through the myriad landscapes of emotion and introspection. It helps me to explore and heal by articulating the intricacies of life through my poetry. I am thrilled to share this exploration with you through this book.

The poems have been written over the past seven years and translated during the past year. It reflects my growth as a person and a poet. Each poem tries to capture the essence of my feelings and reflections during a point in time. From the quiet whispers of nature to the loud clamor of the human heart, these poems span a wide range of themes, including love, loss, hope, introspection, and celebration of life.

In "Boundaries of The Mind," I delve into the struggle for self-realization and the journey from despair to liberation. "The Man in My Lake" reflects on betrayal and the swift changes that can potentially alter one's core values. "Ode to Chairs" personifies an inanimate object, evoking themes of memory, neglect, and the passage of time. "Mother" portrays the essence of motherhood as a gift of immense love and sacrifice. "Lost Echoes of the Earth" laments the loss of connection to nature in the face of modern progress.

I have translated some of the poems into Latin to nurture classical antiquity. A few poems are translated into Hindi and Bangla to reach my extended family who live in various states of India. The translation took much longer than initially anticipated and turned out to be quite a learning experience for me. I hope that readers will be able to connect with the emotions portrayed in the translated version.

Writing poetry is a deeply personal endeavor, yet it tries to bridge the gap between the writer and the readers. I hope that these poems will not only convey my thoughts and feelings but will also inspire you to reflect on your own.

I thank you for embarking on this poetic journey with me. Your readership brings these words to life, and for that, I am profoundly grateful.

With heartfelt appreciation,

Ronok Ghosal

Acknowledgments

I am profoundly grateful to my parents, whose unwavering support in my passion for poetry have been the cornerstone of my creative journey. Their encouragement empowered me to pursue my literary aspirations with determination and resilience. Without their relentless feedback on the translation, it would not have been possible to bring my poems to non-English readers in India.

To my sister, Rhea Ghosal, whose thoughtful critiques and encouragement have been invaluable in shaping my poetry journey. Her insights and enthusiasm have inspired me to continually focus on my revisions. I am immensely grateful for her active participation in improving the readability of the poems.

I extend my heartfelt appreciation to the Poetry Society of Texas for providing a nurturing community where poets thrive, share their work, and collaborate with fellow writers. Their dedication to promoting poetry has created a supportive environment that fosters growth and creativity. I am honored to be a part of such a vibrant literary community.

I would like to extend my heartfelt thanks to Lopamudra Banerjee, an esteemed Indian writer, poet, editor, and translator currently based in Dallas, Texas. Her insightful feedback on my poems has been invaluable in shaping this collection. My deepest gratitude also goes to the entire publishing team at Black Eagle Books, led by Satya Pattanaik, whose dedication and expertise brought this book to life.

Finally, to all the readers who have embraced my poetry, thank you. Your exploration of this book is a testament to the enduring power of poetry to transcend boundaries and touch hearts. I am deeply grateful for your support and hope that my poems continue to resonate with you long after you close this book.

With heartfelt appreciation,

Ronok Ghosal

Table of content

English

Boundaries of The Mind

This poem depicts a journey from despair to liberation. The speaker feels trapped in a shadowed room, isolated, and abandoned, but ultimately discovers inner strength. They realize they are their own savior, breaking free from mental constraints and embracing a new life filled with hope and sanity

Boundaries of The Mind

They told me it would be fine
Everything would come together
Well, wasn't that a huge, blatant lie?
I can expect it certainly never

Trapped alone in the shadowed room
The doors and windows shut so tense
I will be lonely forever I assume
Even if I break out there lies a fence

Why even try when I know there's despair!
The only way to be free is to be saved.
Oh, who would come on the white mare
To help me out of this wretched place?

He never came, nobody seems to care
No, they did, looking right at my face
They said: 'Talk to me if you ever need help'
Why did the violin stay in the case?

Why did it not play, the joy could be felt.
Just take the chance to win the race
Between the demon of thought or tension and I
Standing up, for I will not cry

The knight in the armor was me the whole time
I took the hammer and destroyed my chain
I kicked down the door and ran to the right lane
I broke the fence and headed for the train

And well the train, the train took me where there was no
rain
It took me to a paradise filled with beings sane
A paradise where I renounced old ties, and a new life
emerged.

A Long Life

This poem contemplates the passage of time and the cycle of life, pleading for the sun to rise slowly. It reflects on youth's fleeting nature and the eventual return to the earth. Acknowledging life's impermanence, it emphasizes leaving a meaningful legacy for the future. The sunset symbolizes life's end, yet the poem stresses the enduring impact of one's actions. It urges cherishing each moment and making the most of life's fleeting beauty.

A Long Life

When the sun rises, the earth will glow
Please let it rise oh so slow
When dawn occurred, I begged for no higher
May I delay noon, for I have no desire

Inevitability strikes, midday has begun
Up and up the young man will run
My baby will soon return to where it came
The pleasures of Gaea aren't even close to aim

He has now been long gone
For centuries the sunset has been done.
My child, just know your story cannot be omit
So many births will read to where was your summit

Each day has always mattered
Every night you left trying, yet battered
Months and years of hard effort
But what paid back was the diamond sand in a dessert

At the end what I am trying to say is not complex
The imprint you leave behind will pave way for the next.

The Ferocity of the World's Simplicity

This poem talks about how simple things, like throwing a stone into a lake, can be rough and create big effects. It also looks at why people act violently, even though it doesn't solve anything. The poem asks if everyone can get along peacefully. It says that we need to talk to each other and understand each other's feelings to find solutions. It's about wanting a world where people don't hurt each other and where we all work together to make things better.

The Ferocity of the World's Simplicity

The man throws the pebble in the lake for a ripple tough
Does he act in that certain way because he simply can?
There isn't any reason why his workings need to be so
rough
The shots rang out making, while people randomly ran
As if to answer the question of society's perception of
authority
It is not a question of who will win this altercation,
rightfully they will all
The truth is people must check their own yards to
maintain security

The list of horrors within human communities will make
your skin crawl
Watching the news on the television alongside your
loved ones
Hoping that these acts happening to others broadcasted
will not happen to you
Witnessing it all with my eyes, my heart weighs several
tons
Such terrible things do not happen to a chosen few
My blood would race if I walked in an unfamiliar block
I would escape the location as quickly as I could, but
why would I?

Am I falling from a cliff, landing in the bottom of a
jagged rock?
Is there a reason for fright, from what I have seen in life
with my eyes?
Why can all this violence just not come to a cease?

So many people have asked and asked
Is it even possible to attain peace?
Yes, and it should have been performed attained long in
the past
No matter what your perspective is, think like the
opposition

Violence will not win any argument but intensify it so
fast
Us humans must use the gifts we have,
The gift of precision Communication

Tell the opposing side your side of the narration
To arrive at a middle path, a path of reconciliations
No one will feel the pain of others' frustrations
As we humans will go on building more relations
Living without the knowledge of t our fellow peoples'
humans' aggravation

The Man in My Lake

This poem talks about how simple things, like throwing a stone into a lake, can be rough and create big effects. It also looks at why people act violently, even though it doesn't solve anything. The poem asks if everyone can get along peacefully. It says that we need to talk to each other and understand each other's feelings to find solutions. It's about wanting a world where people don't hurt each other and where we all work together to make things better.

The Man in My Lake

I had crossed mountains and ran through the sand
Days turned to months, months turned to years, I was
still lost of find.
Fooled soul meets a fellow who gives his right hand.
His left hand in his pocket held the victim's mind
We rest at the inn, with innocent calm
Sinister plotting of a torture soon to come
The other man spelled, before they wake at dawn:
"Follow me, I will show where the gold is from!"
The two walked many days and saw
A lake
With sky-blue waters, the depth
He tried to fathom, and recalled …
Mine, this lake was solely mine.
As soon as my sight abandoned the blues,
Looking remotely to the side, absent,
I recollected my beautiful realm of livelihood dark
Where I used to swim,
It was polluted now
Purity of the reflection stained by his mark
The innocence of the portrait swiftly looted
How did my totality change, how so fast?

Passage

This poem describes a father guiding his child through life, like a puppeteer directing a play. The father teaches important lessons as the child grows, but eventually, the child learns to manage on their own. As time passes, the child gains independence, symbolized by the completion of the journey. In the end, the child faces life's challenges armed with the wisdom passed down, ready to make their own choices.

Passage

Just a decade with one ago commenced quaternity
A play whose direction is done by the master puppeteer
He who develops the sacred crowning of paternity
Not once but twice for the pacer to endure
Holds every string to help the puppets grasp
For when they are new to the terrain, they must learn
Hence when swimming in waters of change, they
shouldn't gasp
As time will pass, the spell will brew, row or sink, savor
or yearn
In the cruise of time, the puppets were boarded
to kill the sea monster of time
Passage is current and running the spell is a quarter done
The spell will let puppets bear weapons or die in dirt and
grime
Passage is current and running the spell is half done
Complications of murder are rife; the monster has done
no crime.
Passage is current and running the spell is a quarter done
The puller of strings is there, his forehead filled with
sweat
Time is up.
Passage is current and running the spell is done
The puppets are alive, in their hand's sword or sentence

Providence

This is a poem about how selfish choices bring sorrow and suffering. Even if the wrongdoer doesn't realize it, their actions have consequences. The poem shows that despite trying to avoid punishment, the wrongdoer's deeds will catch up with them. It teaches us that justice always prevails, replacing wickedness with fairness.

Providence

Into the under
The sorrowed souls land into
One selfish blunder
For every dream they dreamt

While the spirit cries in woe
The mighty sails of fate are released
But little does he know
The wrongdoer's torture will inevitably increase

However, the scheme has a flaw
The abhorrent acts will never cease
Unimaginable pain, but no draw
Wicked laughs turn to anguished cries

A misthought deed gets replaced
As the truths of humanity emerge and rise.
Flames of punishment and a mortal face

One no match for the other
As providence in its role is engaged.

The Wanderer's Haven

This poem celebrates the joy of travel and discovery. The poem portrays the wanderer's journey through winding roads and distant lands, fueled by a sense of adventure. Each step unveils new horizons and reveals mysteries, creating a tapestry of priceless tales etched on the earth. As the wanderer encounters diverse cultures and experiences, a harmonious symphony of humanity emerges. Through travel, the wanderer discovers the richness of life's tapestry, unburdened and free to explore.

The Wanderer's Haven

Upon the winding roads meandering into to distant lands,
The whisper of adventure stirs within his body,
New horizons emerge, drawn by unseen hands,
In the embrace of wanderlust, he finds his destiny

The maps unfurl, revealing mysteries,
Each step, a narrative etched on the earth,
Through steep hills and mountains, through oak wood
breeze,
A tapestry of priceless tales takes birth.

In foreign tongues, a harmony takes flight,
A symphony of cultures interweaved,
In each visage of his encounters, a pure bright light
shines,
The nomad's journey, is thus, profoundly conceived.

So let him roam, unburdened free,
In his travel exploits, he unveils life's tapestry.

Creation of Creation

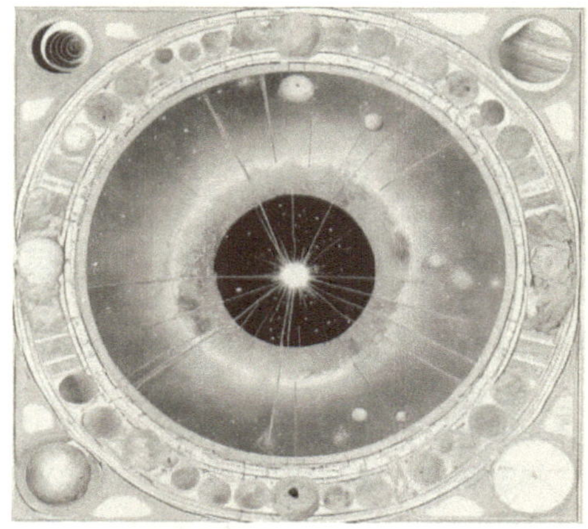

This poem talks about how the universe began and evolved over time. It describes how, billions of years ago, there was a big explosion, like the sound of a needle dropping. This explosion led to the formation of stars and planets, which became homes for many living things, including us. But eventually, stars and planets die, which is a natural part of the universe's life cycle. So, the poem reflects on how everything in the universe, including us, is connected and how life and death are part of this amazing process.

Creation of Creation

Time on time until the series will stop.
Thirteen three thousand ago time absent
It seemed like the burst of a needle drop
The booming sound, the enchantment of infinite bombs

Then came spheres the size of suns and larger
Crashing rapidly like raging giant bulls
Parties of burning stars spiraling into the dark voids

The life of homes for billions staging
The homes for us eight three thousands then ployed
The graced house taken for granted aging
Her death and her attraction kills a nemesis
She dies her death, a murder by idol
The creation of our creation killed

A Confusing World

This is an **Acrostic** poem, which delves into the disorientation and frustration experienced by someone grappling with memory loss, due to dementia. Each day passes into the next, with visitors recounting tales that feel unfamiliar and distant. They seek solace in music, a familiar comfort amidst the confusion. Despite feeling like a stranger in their own life, they find a moment of clarity and connection through a cherished memory of hearing music.

A Confusing World

Days tick away like the clock on my wall
Every single day people come to my bed
Making up stories that I don't cannot recall
Expecting me to believe what they said.

Night falls and I hum a song, playing the guitar

Then they come in and look at me
I look away at those unfamiliar sorrowful faces,
All behaving they know me for ages.

They treat me as if I'm a baby boy

Operating Chiding me, coaxing me, like I always need
help

Regardless, I listen, there is no choice
My bedroom is my sanctuary where l dwell

Except for one day when I heard music
Noiselessly I crept out of bed to see
The gentle strumming of the soft acoustics
Singing along to an old memory.

Reality Avenue

This poem contemplates the superiority between different eras, possibly the past ("Titan era") and the present ("new age"). The poem explores themes of power, chaos, and transformation. It reflects on the evolution of humanity and the complexities of existence. The imagery of chaos in the mind and the contrast between light and darkness symbolize the struggles and uncertainties of life. Ultimately, the poem suggests that despite the challenges and madness of the present, the "new age" is deemed superior to the past.

Reality Avenue

Titan era or the new age, which was more superior.?

God were children,
babies to power,
fire to bomb.

Everyday chaos in the brain,
body and mind overlap in time-lapse.
Ending for the painting of waning.
Waxing and waning of a new light in the making.
Space-ache caused the waking of the light,
The lingering harmony of cream clouds in waters.

Thirteen billion,
for doorways to form,
only few takings exist in medium.
Right or wrong better gone than chaos fields,
where the grass is blue and the sky dull green.
Uprooting the depth of what hadn't lurked,

but screaming in joy of
the madness felt.

The new age proven superior to the times back then.

Ode to Chairs

This poem celebrates the silent companionship of a neglected chair, adorned in a suit of dust yet dignified in its posture. Despite its stoic appearance, it carries the weight of memories from years past, when it served faithfully amidst abandonment. The chair, once a staple of daily life, now languishes in solitude, yearning for recognition and empathy. As it waits patiently for a reunion with its long-lost family, the poem contemplates the inevitability of decay and the bittersweet prospect of eternal rest.

Ode to Chairs

Finely postured,
wearing a suit
of dust

You sat without a trace of movement.
Lonely, yet fierce as a wolf.

The somber piece of furniture crafted with oak.

Now sits as a misfit
in the automobile house.

The magnitude of its vintage appeal increases day by day

Its memories resurface, memories of the first decade past
the second millennia.

It was used every day,
when everyday else was abandoned in the last six years.
And now, it lies, sobbing, covered in spider's net.

Oh, how it has missed me.!
While I have not given it a single thought.
It yearned for empathy,
waiting patiently,

sitting on the cold floor with the hot air.
Did it receive its only glimpse of freedom,
when the car's door was lifted, revealing a dungeon.?
Perhaps, one day its long-lost family will grace its
burden.
With the burden of their weight, on its fine cushion.

That day he will feel comfort after prolonged
restlessness.
However, if this day
never arrives,
It will bear an eternity
of pain.

The legs will buckle,
filth will seep in.

The poor chair living with its family for over half a
decade ago,
will enter the domain of eternal sleep.
Without a memory to keep its long-lost legacy.

Always the Same

This poem talks about how life often feels repetitive, like a broken watch stuck at twelve. Even though there are sometimes surprises, things often come back around in the same way. The poem suggests that even when we want change, we end up sticking to what we know. It's like walking the same path repeatedly, using the same old stick, wondering if there's any point in trying to break free from this cycle when they're comfortable where they are.

Always the Same

The gear inside of my watch has broken
The old clock remains at twelve, stuck and stead
At six this morning no one had woken-
At twelve I stretched my arms up and went to bed

In life the same things come back in rotation
There are, however, times when I get an occasional
surprise

But all shooting stars have constellations

And to pay for any gift we must pay a price.
My mind mirrors the monotonous tick
And I walk a trail carved by prior strolls
I always hike using the same old stick
The morning's heat balanced with the night's cold

What's the reason to bring change, or break a barrier
When I'm content, resting in a glum state?
Isn't the heavy weight of life held by one carrier
The perpetual cycle of fate?

Echoes of Corona

This poem critiques the human response to the COVID-19 pandemic, highlighting the irony of complaining about nature's state while previously neglecting its beauty. The poem suggests that before the pandemic, people often stayed indoors despite fresh air and outdoor opportunities, always glued to their phones. Now, amidst lockdowns and restrictions, they complain about their situation, but the poem questions whether they truly appreciate the consequences of their past actions. It implies that their current suffering may be a result of their previous disregard for nature and karma.

Echoes of Corona

You sulk and wail, that you are not enjoying nature's
traits
but before, nature wasn't so great

You would stay at home when the air was fresh
What did you enjoy, is there a need to guess?

The sun and grass were overlooked necessities
Now sit and reminisce about outdoor festivities

Now suffering in what we think is pain
And sitting alone looking outside in disdain

Mother

This poem is dedicated to my mother and all mothers. The poem celebrates the importance of mothers and the gift of life they give. It talks about how being a mother involves both challenges and joys. Despite the difficulties, mothers play a vital role in nurturing and raising their children. The poem highlights the special bond between a mother and her child, showing how it's like an essential part of a beautiful castle.

Mother

The perennial existence of an annual celebration

symbol of debt in essence, more than a celebration.

Debt not to give for the reason of legation
But given for the reason for the righteous set
A decade and three and then two for twice later
A gift so large no other is larger
Placing new beings on lustrous nature
The giver radiating such warmth, fairer than the sun

The thought of the start of life
Such a privilege, it wouldst burn the mind

For the first for two later the gift bore no lack of strife
The giver did not cry but remained its own kind
The same occurred for the second two later the gift was
oh so grim

The gift, eyes open, but oh so blind

The first started to see, but skimmed the surroundings
No one will realize how the giver, the nurturer mattered
with ascertainment

The giver will only know as she has lived through it all.
From horrendous cries to the horrendous scent
From utter stubbornness to a gift that grew

Now the gift seems to fit in the cupboard

However, the cupboard's part of a castle, maintained by
you.

Before the Horizon

This poem reminisces about a past filled with brightness and laughter, where time seemed weightless and carefree. The poem describes the emergence of the sun as a symbol of hope and cherished memories. Despite the passage of time, the speaker longs to recapture the magic of those days, now overshadowed by the relentless march of time. They yearn to mend fractured bonds and preserve fleeting moments in their hearts. The poem evokes a sense of nostalgia and longing for a time before life's complexities became overwhelming.

Before the Horizon

In the bygone days, life's tapestry so bright,
We waltzed through time, unburdened by its weight.
The sun emerged, dispelling the endless night,

In its rays, it carried the cherished echoes of a vanished
state.
Laughter flowed like rivers, winding through light,
Each second, gems plucked from the morrow's chest.
The ballet of the time clouded our sight,
We waltzed with the sun, our skins the sun rays caressed.

Time strides on, a thief, unseen in its flight,
Stealing hours, casting shadows without haste.
So, our hearts, magnets, hope to reunite,
To mend fractured bonds - memories encased.

We dream of days when life was but a jest,
In our hearts that ache for moments to persist.
A gallery of thoughts, we find our rest,
In a time before the horizon's crest

Winter's Warmth

This poem describes the beauty of winter, with snow covering everything like a sparkling blanket. The falling snowflakes create a magical scene, and the twinkling lights add to the charm. Despite the cold outside, the warmth of a cozy fire brings people together. The poem shows how, during winter's cold, love and togetherness can make everything feel warm and special.

Winter's Warmth

In winter's grasp, the world is cloaked in white,
A canvas, sparkling, ever pure and bright.
When snowflakes fall, like diamonds in the night,
They paint a scene of wonder and delight.

The lights, like stars, in the cold night's embrace,
Twinkle and dance, as if in a celestial race.
Their glow transforms the frosty, barren space,
Cold white streams spiral downwards, like Skyfall,
leaving a delicate trace

Yet in our homes, a fire's warm, gentle blaze,
It battles the chill of those frosty days.
Drawing us close, in its inviting ways,
Cozy hearths, and love's familiar rays,
Winter's allure, a marvel to behold.

With snow and lights, it weaves tales untold.
But by the fire, we find a love so bold,
In contrast, we discover life's pure gold.

Lost Echoes of the Earth

This poem laments how we're forgetting about nature as cities grow and technology advances. Even though nature is all around us, we often ignore it because we're too focused on our screens and busy lives. The poem asks if we still notice the beauty of mountains and oceans, or if we're too busy polluting them. It reminds us to appreciate nature's gifts before they're gone.

Lost Echoes of the Earth

Amidst the urban hum, where progress gleams
A symphony of nature softly weaves
Each leaf and bloom, a life that thrives and believes lives
Yet is drowned by progress, lost in modern streams

Beneath the city lights, is there a starry night?
A canvas painted with celestial fire?
But in our screens, we seek what does inspire
The beauty missed, eclipsed by artificial light

Majestic mountains, silent guardians
With lofty peaks, untouched, in grand repose
Yet overlooked, they remain, as ambition blindly grows
In nature's arms, a solace rarely pardons

The oceans dance with waves that kiss the shore
A ballet of tides, an endless embrace
Yet we pollute the earth, leaving scars we can't erase
Forgetting nature's gifts, craving for more and more

In every rustling tree and murmuring breeze
A whisper of a truth we seldom hear
Nature's beauty, pure and crystal clear
Yet in our haste, do we let it silently appease?

My Dove

The poem captures the tranquility of mornings awakened by the gentle tweeting of a dove and the beauty of nature's awakening. However, as the day transitions into night, the comforting presence of the dove becomes a poignant reminder of life's fleeting moments. The poem reflects on the inevitability of change and the eventual departure of the dove, symbolizing the transient nature of all things. Despite the certainty of the dove's departure, its song remains a cherished memory, echoing in the stillness of the night.

My Dove

I wake up to the sound of my dove tweeting
To the crisp morning light flooding through
To beautiful days enhanced with the garden's aroma
The body of the grass shining with dewdrops
But all of this disappears
when the sun sets
I know that
whether the Night brings rain
Or shouts in rage
My little birdie will wake me in the morning
Twittering, chirping
Always on the twelfth branch
of the same pine tree

But what comes with the day
When will my songbird leave?
A bird can only stay for so long
until it's time
for the song to end
and the music to fade

Until there is nothing
that can wake me from the night.

A Crowded Coffee Shop

This poem explores the contradiction between the bustling atmosphere of the café and the perceived shortcomings within. Despite its shabby appearance, bitter coffee, and indifferent staff, the café is packed with people. The poem ends with the themes of disconnection and existential uncertainty.

A Crowded Coffee Shop

I arrived at a café
Navigating my way
Finding it at the start of south street.
I walk inside
The interiors look shabby
the coffee tastes bitter
the waiters appear rude
and the options seem few
but the shop is crowded
So crowded I can't see vacant space
I can't help but wonder
"Why are there so many people in a place like this?"
I try to ask them
For what reasons they picked this coffee shop
Their eyes don't meet mine
Not a single soul responds

All of them, quiet as a grave
and then
I try to remember
"How did I get here?"

Everywhere I Look

This poem is about feeling the presence of a lost loved one everywhere in nature. Memories of them are found in the whispers of trees, the soaring eagles, and the flowing rivers. Even among the stars, they seek comfort but find only silence, highlighting the deep sense of loss.

Everywhere I Look

Amidst trees, your whispers so softly speak,

Memories linger through leaves, tense shadows glare,

Carving wounds, time can't erase, sorrows seek,
A heavy heart, laden with care you bear.
On Over the mountain peaks, eagles freely soar,

Your spirit lingers in crisp mountain air.
You carry the weight of sorrow a burden hard to explore,
Heart heavy, laden with the weight you bear.

Beside the river's flow, a winding stream,
Reflections of your laughter, a distant dream.
Crisp waves of grief persist, like water's endless gleam,
An unrelenting current, of your spirit beams.

In fields of green, wildflowers gently bloom,
Your absence paints meadows in pale hues.
Symphony of sorrow, a mournful tune,
Nature weeps, as if she, too might lose.

Among the stars, in the vast expanse, rising high,
I seek your face in constellations bright.
Cosmic silence muffles my every cry,
Echo of despair in a soundless night.

In every corner of this world, you're found,
Your haunting presence in every step I take.
Yet relentless grip of your grief, a heavy mound,
A journey through a mourning heart, we make.

In shadows deep, where sorrow finds its home
A tender light, a glimmer, softly gleams
Though absence lingers, you are not alone
In memories, love's flame forever beams.

An Urban Serenade

This poem talks about the clash between city life and nature's beauty. It says that even though nature is all around us, we often ignore it because we're too focused on our screens and busy lives. The poem reminds us that nature is important, and we should take the time to appreciate it. It mentions how we sometimes forget about the damage we're doing to the environment by polluting and destroying it. It tells us to listen to nature's whispers and enjoy its beauty before it's gone.

An Urban Serenade

Amidst the urban hum, where progress gleams
A symphony of nature softly weaves
Each leaf and bloom, a poem that believes
Yet drowned by progress, lost in modern streams

Beneath the city lights, a starry night
A canvas painted with celestial fire
But in our screens, we seek what does inspire
The beauty missed, eclipsed by artificial light
Majestic mountains, silent guardians

Their lofty peaks, untouched, in grand repose
Yet overlooked, as ambition blindly grows
In nature's arms, a solace rarely pardon.
The oceans dance with waves that kiss the shore
A ballet of tides, an endless embrace

Yet we pollute, leaving scars we can't erase
Forgetting nature's gifts, craving more and more
In every rustling tree and rustling breeze
A whisper of a truth we seldom hear
Nature's beauty, pure and crystal clear
Yet in our haste, we let it silently appease

Hues and Hazes

This poem celebrates the beauty of summer, describing the pleasant scents of flowers and the warm sunlight. It paints a picture of joyful meadows and peaceful moments, where worries seem to fade away. The poem suggests that summer brings a sense of freedom and renewal, as nature's colors and scents fill us with happiness and calm. It's a time to enjoy the simple pleasures and appreciate the beauty of the world around us.

Hues and Hazes

The scent of flowers, permeate the summer breeze,
Their fragrant whispers linger in the air,
The sun's warm touch, a gentle, soft caress,
A symphony of joy beyond compare.

The meadows dance with golden hues so bright,
The joyous spirit of nature fills the balmy afternoon,
Each moment bathed in pure and sheer delight,
In happiness, we find our sweetest tune.

The scent of pine and ocean in the breeze,
With every breath, a sense of peace descends,
In sunlight's kiss, the soul finds a divine release,
And all life's worries seem to meet their ends.

In summer's grasp, the soul finds sweet release,
As warmth pervades, dispelling winter's chill,
A buoyant spirit, dancing in the breeze,
In golden moments, time stands hushed and still.

What Really Comes to Be

This poem explores the contrast between dreams and reality. In the night, dreams take flight, painting a beautiful picture of possibilities. However, when dawn breaks, reality can be harsh and unforgiving, revealing the truth behind our illusions. Despite the challenges, there is beauty to be found in the chaos of reality, like a phoenix rising from the ashes. The poem encourages us to embrace both dreams and reality, finding solace and beauty in the fleeting moments of life.

What Really Comes to Be

In night's luscious ballet, dreams take flight,
In a tapestry of hues, in a symphony of lights.
The dawn arrives with its relentless might,
And unveils reality's stark, unforgiving sight.
In the twilight's whispered symphony,
Where dreams shine like stars in cosmic harmony,

Morning's revelation, a harsh decree,
Unravels illusions in its clarity.
O, reality, in your labyrinth of thorns,
Dreams are tangled, hopes are torn.
Yet, within the chaos, new beauty born,
A phoenix rising from the ashes, reborn.

Come, let us navigate this maze, this rhyme,
Embrace the fleeting dreams, the whispers of time.
In their ephemeral grace, we find the sublime,
A refuge from reality's relentless chime.

A Seaside

This poem reflects on life's journey through the lens of the sea. One on deathbed, finds solace. The waves symbolize the passage of time, carrying tales of the past and the memories that shaped their life. The sands serve as a testament to both joy and pain experienced throughout life. As the sea mirrors life's ebb and flow, one finds acceptance and peace as they near the end of their journey. With the salty air as their final embrace, they bid farewell to the world, embracing the promise of a new beginning

A Seaside

Upon my deathbed by the Italian shore,
My intent gaze falls on the waves, life's myriad tales
they pour.
Each ripple whispers secrets of my past,
Moments that were cherished, moments that didn't last.
The sands beneath, a chronicle in grain,
Each granule tells a story, a saga of joy and pain.

The sea, a mirror of life's ebb and flow,
Reflects the human journey I've come to know.
Like its waves that rise and fall, my memories rise,
And crash upon the shore, beneath the skies.
The salty air, a bittersweet embrace,
As life's finale nears, I find my place.

In this s pristine seaside's gentle sigh,
I find acceptance as the tides draw nigh.
With my last precious breath, I bid the world adieu.
Embracing peace as a fresh life begins anew.

Whispers of Warmth

This poem captures the intimate connection between human emotions and nature's beauty. The poem describes a summer day filled with vivid sensory details, portraying the warmth and tranquility of the season. It contrasts the longing of winter with the joy of the present moment, emphasizing the comfort found in nature's embrace. Through imagery of fields, flowers, and evening serenades, the poem highlights the deep harmony and shared secrets between us and the natural world, celebrating the enduring warmth and beauty that nature brings to human life.

Whispers of Warmth

Sweet light, orange nectar, and a warm haze
The warm rain painted your front lawn
I see you crystal clear in the dew drops
But I could close my eyes and know you came

Through winter's frost, I dreamed of this embrace
Fireflies dance in the dusky air
Among wildflowers, we find our solace
A season's breath holds secrets we will share

Golden fields wave hello in the soft breeze
Sunflowers turn to greet the dawn
The scent of jasmine fills the evening air
Echoes of laughter drift across the lawn

As twilight deepens, stars begin to gleam
Crickets sing their serenade sweet
In every shadow, nature's touch is seen
With every heartbeat, her warmth we meet

The Museum of Memories

This poem portrays the solitary journey through a metaphorical museum filled with memories of a lost love. Each exhibit and artwork symbolize different aspects of their relationship, from the vibrant joy of shared moments to the somber realization of its end. Despite the passage of time and the fading of tangible connections, the presence and essence of the loved one remain vividly alive in the speaker's heart and memories, underscoring the everlasting nature of true emotional bonds.

The Museum of Memories

In corridors of memories, I stroll alone,
A museum vast, where echoes softly sigh,
Each exhibit whispers tales of love, now flown,
In galleries of heart, your memory's nigh.

A canvas once adorned with laughter's gleam,
Now hangs in somber hues, its brilliance waned,
Brushstrokes of joy, now lost within a dream,
Yet in my soul, your image still remained.

A sculpture stands, once carved, our bond so strong,
Now stands forsaken, in the shadows cast,
Its form now cold, its meaning now beyond,
A monument to love that couldn't last.

Yet in this gallery, your presence beams,
In every corner of my heart, it seems-
That though you're gone, your essence still prevails,
In memories, your touch forever sails

Latin

Fin es Animi
(Boundaries of the Mind)

Fin es Animi

Omnia ut conveniant
Nonne erat magnum mendacium
Exspectare id certe possum numquam
Captae solae in umbrosa loca
Ostia et fenestrae quam tentae clauduntur
possum me assumere solum esse in aeternum
Etiamsi erumpam ibi sepes iacet
Cur etiam temptam, cum desperationem ibi esse scio
liber esse solus est salvari
o quis veniet in candida equa
Adiuva me miserum ex hoc loco
Numquam venit, nemo curare videtur
Non -- curarunt, vultus ad faciem meam
Loquere ad me, si semper opus est auxilio
Cur vita mansit apud buxem
Cur non lusit -- gaudium nonne sentiri?
modo accipe forte vincere in stadio
Inter daemonem cogitationis vel contentionis et ego
Stans quoniam non clamabo
ego eram miles in armis toto tempore
Ego malleum et catenam meam cepi
calcitravi ostiumEt dixit mihi id facturum esse
bonum   et cucurri ad dextram venellam
Fregi saepem et pergeret ad agmen
hamaxostichus et bene me tamen tulit ubi pluuius non
erat
Paradisus repletus fiendi et sanus
paradisus renuntiatus est tamquam si nova vita

Ode Cathedras
(Ode to Chairs)

Ode Cathedras

Pulchre positae;
gerens sectam
terrenam.
Sedisti sine vestigio motus.
Tam solitarius quam lupus.
Flebilis querco facta supellex.
Nunc est quae sedet
in automobile domum.
Perusa, vindemiae in dies auget magnitudinem.
Memoriae primi decennii praeteriti secundi millennii
est.de
Quotidie usa est;
quando quotidie finivit in ultimis sex annis?
Ululans, araneis rete velata ;
o, quomodo me omisit.
Donec non aliquam ipsi dedi.
empathiaeque cupida;
patienter exspectans;
sedens in pavimento frigido cum aere calido.
Unicum suum perceptionem libertatis recipiens;
cum porta carceris portatur.
Una dies, si familia amissa diuturnum feret onus.
Sarcina ponderis, in pulvinari tenui.
Tunc solacium tantae longae inquietudinis persentiscet.
Sed si haec dies
numquam advenit;

portabit aeternum
vitam doloris.
Crura fibula erunt;
sordes pereffluet
Tum sella pauperis cum familia sua tantum supra
dimidium decennium habitabat;
eternum intrabit somnum.
Sine memoria longam amissam legatum servare.

Ubique aspicio
(Everywhere I look)

Ubique aspicio

Inter arbores, tibi tam molliter loquuntur susurri;
Per folia, memorias effluunt umbrae tentus fulgor.
Vulnera, tempus abolere non potest, dolores quaerunt;
Gravis cor, onustus cura quae gerimus.
In verticibus montium aquilae sponte considunt
advolantque;
Tuus animus in rigido montium moratur aere.
Doloris pondus, onus difficile explorare;
Cor gravis, onustus pondere quod gerimus.
Iuxta ipsius fluminis cursum, torrens torrens;
Risum cogita, somnium longinquum.
Rigent undae luctus, ceu lux perennis aquae;
Perseverans, currens, implacabilis, tigna.
In pratis viridibus flosculae leniter florent;
Tua nunc absentia pingit pallentia prata colore.
Symphonia moeroris, lugubris modulatio;
Natura flet, ut si ipsa quoque amittat.
Inter sidera, vasto in alto;Vultum tuum in sideribus
quaero.
Mundi silentium obumbrat omnem clamorem;
in Nocte tacita desperationis Echo.
In omni angulo huius mundi inventus es;
obsidens praesentia in quisque gradu
At tumulus gravis urget dolor ;
Iter per corde lugubri facimus.
In altis umbris, ubi dolor domum suam invenitiu
Lumen tenerum, sublustris, molliter relucet
Etsi absentia cunctatur, solus non es
In memoriam, flamma amoris in perpetuum fulget

Serenata Urbana

(An Urban Serenade)

Serenata Urbana

Inter urbana murmura, ubi inaestuat progressus
Symphonia naturae molliter texit
Quisque folium et flos, poema quae credit!
Progressu tamen submersa, in recentibus rivis amissa
Luminibus sub urbis, nox siderea
Carbasus igne caelesti depictus
In nostris autem pluteis quaerimus quid inspirat
Pulchritudo perita, eclipsatur per lucubrationem
Magnifici montes, taciti custodes
Alta cacumina, intacta, magna quies
Sed neglecta, cum temere crescit ambitio
In armis naturae raro solatium remissum.
Oceani saltant fluctus, qui osculantur litus
Aestuum talarium, inexhaustum amplexum
At nos polluimus, cicatrices quae abolere non possumus
donorum naturae obliviscimus, magis magisque cupiens
In omni ligno crepitante ac crepitante aura
Susurra veritatis raro audimus
Pulchritudo naturae, pura et liquida
Sed festinantes tacite id dimittimus placare

Ante horizontem
(Before the horizon)

Ante horizontem

Olim, vitae peripetasmata tam clara;
Spatiamur per temporem, non onerati pondere.
Sol emersit, noctemque sine fine removit;
Echo amata status evanescentis
Risus fluebat ut flumina flexa per lumen;
Alterum, gemmae crastina pectore decerptae.
Tabernaculum ricini obnubilavit conspectum nostrum;
saltare valsam cum solis radii blandiuntur cupimus.
tempus ingradior, fur, in fuga latens;
Horas furans, umbras sine festinatione mittens.
Sic magnetes corda reunire sperant;
Vincula fractis sarcire -- Memorias languescentes.
Somniamus dierum, quibus vita fuit iocum modo;
In cordibus dolentibus momentis perseverandis
Porticus cogitationum, requiem nostram invenimus
In tempore ante horizontis cristam

Hindi

मन की सीमा
(Boundaries of the mind)

मन की सीमा

वो कहते थे, सब ठीक हो जाएगा
वो कहते थे, सब कुछ ठीक है
तो क्या वो एक बड़ा झूठ था
मुझे इसकी नहीं थी उम्मीद

छायामय अंधकार घर में कैद
बंद दरवाज़े और खिड़कियों में, मैं निःसंग
इसे लंघन करने पे, हैं बाधा और भी
अवसाद में सोचु, व्यर्थ क्यों करे प्रयास
मुक्ति का एकमात्र उपाय, कोई यदि करे उद्धार

सफेद घोड़े पर आएगा कौन
इस अत्याचारित प्राण को दिलाने मुक्ति
वो कभी नहीं आया?
आया था, मेरे सामने था खड़ा
मुझे उत्साहित करके बोला था - "करो आह्वान उसे"

सारंगी क्यों रह गई अपनी कोष में
निःशब्दता में खो गया स्पर्श आनंद का

अंत में सोचा, एहि हैं वो जय का स्वर्ण सुयोग
चिंता और अस्थिरता के बीच खड़ा हूँ मैं

नहीं करूँगा अब और अश्रु विसर्जन
समझ गया मैं, की कवच पहने वह सेनापति मैं ही हूँ

अस्त्र चलाकर किया ध्वंश मैंने बन्धनों का
गया मैं पकड़ने सपनों का रेल, तोरकर अव्सदो का द्वार
जो ले जाएगा थकानभरी वर्षा से बहुत दूर
विपन्न जीवन की आहुति देकर, पूर्ण लोकप्रिय जग में
नए जीवन की खोज में

अस्तित्व
(A Long Life)

अस्तित्व

सुर्योदय पे होती है पृथ्वी प्रकाशित

विनती हैं की धीरे धीरे ही उठे ऊपर वो

हो गया सवेरा, उसे और ऊपर उठने की जरूरत है नहीं

दोपहर की नहीं है कोई चाह

अनिवार्य मध्याहन हो गया है शुरू

युवा का शुरू हो गया है दौड़

बच्चे आएंगे वापस अपने घर

लक्ष्य हैं नहीं निकट

वह चला गया बहुत पहले ही

सूर्यास्त है अनवरत

संतान जानता है, तुम्हारी कहानी खो नहीं जाएगी

कई जन्मों तक चलेगा पता तुम्हारे शिखर का

हर दिन है महत्वपूर्ण

हर रात का प्रयास जाता है व्यर्थ

बहुत समय की कठिन मेहनत

रेगिस्तान में मिलती है हीरे की रेत

जो मैं कहने की कोशिश कर रहा हूँ वह है नहीं जटिल

आजके कदम करेंगे प्रशस्त अगले जन्म के मार्ग

मेरी झील में व्यक्ती
(The Man in my lake)

मेरी झील में व्यक्ती

मैंने पहाड़ों को किया है पार, दौड़ा हूँ रेगिस्तान में

दिन बदल गए महीनों में, महीने सालों में

जो मैं ढूंढ रहा था वो है अब भी खोया हुआ

धोखा दिया गया मन को मिला एक साथी, जिसने बढ़ाया अपना

दाहिना हाथ

जेब में था बायां हाथ, उसके शिकार को नियंत्रित करता हुआ

मैं महल में शांति से करता हूं विश्राम

जल्द ही आ रहा है क्रूर षड्यंत्र

उसने भोर से पहले कहा

"मेरा अनुसरण करो, मैं दिखाऊंगा तुम्हें स्रोत सोने का"

कई दिनों की पैदल यात्रा के बाद दो पथिकों ने देखा

एक झील

आकाश के रंग का नीला पानी, जिसकी गहराई

याद आया मुझे - यह हैं मेरी

यह झील थी केवल मेरी

नीले रंग के संकेत ने कर दिया चकाचौंध

वह है अनुपस्थित, बहुत दूर, चला गया निम्न स्थान पे

मेरा सुंदर जीवनपीठ हो गया अंधेरा

मेरा तैराकी स्थल हो गया दूषित

उसकी उपस्थिति में प्रतिबिंब की शुद्धता हो गई धुंधला

लुट गई मूर्ति की शुद्धता

पूरी तरह से गया बदल मैं, इतनी जल्दी?

यात्रापथ

(Passage)

यात्रापथ

एक दशक पहले हुआ था चालू चारपद
प्रमुख निर्देशक द्वारा निर्देशित एक नाटक
वो करते पात्रत्व का पवित्र मुकुट पूर्ण
पहले नहीं दूसरी बार में हुए वो प्रियतम
नए भूखंड में होगा सीखना उन्हें अवश्य
परिवर्तन के जल में बिना थके होगा तैरना
समय के विस्तारित प्रभाव में होगा तैरना या डूबना
मिलेगा उन्हें उनका उपहार या होंगे वो आकुल
पुतले पे करके वश, किया वध समुद्रिक दानव का
हुआ समाप्त यात्रा-पथ का चतुर्थ चरण
पुतले करेंगे अस्त्र-ग्रहण या होगी उनकी मृत्यु
हुआ समाप्त यात्रा-पथ का अर्ध चरण
हत्या हुई जटिल क्योंकि सागर-के दानव ने नहीं किया कोई
अपराध
यात्रा-पथ में रहा बाकी एक चौथा चरण
कपाल में पसीना लिए निर्देशक का समय हुआ खत्म
यात्रा-पथ हुआ समाप्त
जीवित पुत्तुले के हाथ में रही तलवार या हुए सभी दंडित

एक परिणाम
(A Consequence)

एक परिणाम

रोते हुए तुम कहते हो, प्रकृति की आनंद नहीं ले रहे हो तुम

लेकिन कुछ क्षण पहले प्रकृति थी नहीं ऐसी

तुम बंध रहे घर पे, जब हवा के झोंको में था बहार

किया तुमने उपभोग?

अपरिहार्य था तुम्हारे लिए फोन

लेने के बजाय प्रकृति के आनंद

इसलिए अब

भोग रहे हो दुःख

कर्म ने फेरी तुम्हारे प्रति असंतोष की दृष्टि

लेकिन यही तो हैं तुम्हारा उपहार

Bangla

মনের সীমানা
(Boundaries of the mind)

মনের সীমানা

তারা বলেছিল, সব ঠিক হয়ে যাবে
তারা বলেছিল, সবকিছু ঠিক আছে
তাহলে তা কি সবই বড় মিথ্যা ছিল
আমি করতে পারিনাই এটি প্রত্যাশা

ছায়াময় অন্ধকার ঘরে আক্রান্ত
বদ্ধ দরজা এবং জানালায়, আমি নি:সঙ্গ
প্রত্যাবর্তন করলে আছে বাধা আরও
অবসাদ মাঝে বৃথা করা চেষ্টা
মুক্তির একমাত্র উপায় কেউ যদি করে উদ্ধার

সাদা ঘোড়ায় কে আসবে
এই অত্যাচারিত প্রান্ত থেকে দিতে মুক্তি আমাকে
সে কখনো আসেনি?
এসেছিল, আমার সামনে ছিল দাঁড়িয়ে
বলেছিলো করতে আহ্বান তাকে

বেহালা কেন রইলো নিজের কোষে
নিঃশব্দটায়ে গেল হারিয়ে স্পর্শ আনন্দের

অবশেষে ভাবিলাম এই সেই জয়ের স্বর্ণসুযোগ
চিন্তা এবং অস্থিরতার মাঝে দাঁড়িয়ে আমি
করবোনা আর অশ্রুবিসর্জন
বুঝিলাম অচেনা পথের বর্ম পরা সেনাপতি, সেই আমি

হাতুড়ি চালনায় করলাম নিজের বাঁধন ধ্বংস
গেলাম ধরতে স্বপ্নের রেল, গুড়িয়ে অবসাদের দ্বার
যে নিয়ে যাবে ক্লান্তিকর বৃষ্টি থেকে বহুদূর
বিপন্ন জীবনের আহুতি দিয়ে, পূর্ণ জনপ্রিয় জগতে
নতুন জীবনের প্রান্তে

অস্তিত্ব

(A Long Life)

অস্তিত্ব

ওঠে সূর্য, আলোকিত হয়ে পৃথিবী
উঠুক সে ধীরে
ভোর হয়েছে, চাহিনা সে উঠুক আরও ওপরে
নেই কোনো চাহিদা মধ্যাহ্ন-র
অপরিহার্য মধ্যবেলা হলো শুরু
শুরু হলো দৌড় তরুনের
ফিরবে আমার শিশু নিজের উৎসে
লক্ষের সান্নিধ্যে নেই পার্থিব সুখ
গেছে সে চলে বহু আগে
হয়েছে সূর্যাস্ত অবিরাম
জানে আমার সন্তান, তোমার গল্প যাবে না দেওয়া বাদ
বহু জন্ম জানবে তোমার শৃঙ্গের ঠিকানা
গুরুত্বপূর্ণ দিন প্রতিটি
যায় বৃথা প্রতি রাতের প্রয়াস
বহু সময়ের কঠিন প্রচেষ্টা
পাওনা যে শুধু মরুতে হিরার বালি
জটিল নয় বলার চেষ্টা করি যা
আপনার পদক্ষেপ করবে পথ প্রশস্ত পরবর্তী প্রজন্মের

একটি মানুষ আমার হ্রদে
(The Man in my lake)

একটি মানুষ আমার হ্রদে

আমি করেছি পাহাড় অতিক্রম, ছুটেছি মরুতে
পরিণত হলো দিনগুলো মাসে, মাস গুলো বছরে
যা খুঁজি তা রইলো এখনো হারিয়ে
প্রতারিত মন পেলো এক সঙ্গী, যে বাড়ালো তার দান হাথ
আর বাম হাত ছিলো পকেটে নিয়ন্ত্রণ করে তার শিকার
করি দালানে বিশ্রাম নিষ্পাপ শান্তির মাঝে
আসিতেছে শীঘ্রই কুটিলের নৃশংসতা ষড়যন্ত্র
ভোরের আগে বলিলো সে
“করো অনুসরণ আমাকে, দেখাবো সোনার উৎস তোমাকে”
বহু দিন হাটার পর দুই পথিক দেখিলো
একটি হ্রদ
আকাশ বর্ণ নীল জল, গভীরতা যার
স্মরণ করে দেখি যে - আমার
এই হ্রদটি ছিল একমাত্র আমার
দৃষ্টিবিকল করলো পরিত্যাগ নীলের আভাস
পাশে নজর বুঝিলো সে অনুপস্থিত, সে ছিলো বহু দূরত্বে, নিম্নান্তরে
অন্ধকারময় হলো আমার সুন্দর জীবনপীঠ
আমার সন্তরণ স্থল হলো দূষিত
প্রতিবিম্বের পরিশুদ্ধতা হলো ধূসর তার উপস্থিতিতে
প্রতিমূর্তির শুদ্ধতা গেলো দ্রুত লুটে
সমগ্র ভাবে হলাম পরিবর্তন, এত দ্রুত?

যাত্রাপথ
(Passage)

যাত্রাপথ

এক দশকের আগে হয়েছিল চালু চারপদ
প্রধান পরিচালক পরিচালিত একটি নাট্য
করে সে পরিপূর্ণ পাত্রত্বের পবিত্র মুকুট
প্রথমে নয়ে দ্বিতীয় বারে হয়ে সে প্রিয়তম
নতুন ভূখণ্ডে শিখতে হবে তাদের অবশ্যই
পরিবর্তনের জলে কাটলে সাঁতার না হাপায়ে যেন তারা
সময়ের সাথে বিস্তারিত প্রভাবে
টানবে সে দাঁড় বা যাবে সে ডুবে
পাবে তার পাওনা বা হবে সে আকুল
সময়ের পাল, করে ভর পুতুলে, করলো সে বধ সাগর-এর দানব
যাত্রাপথের প্রভাবে হলো শেষ চতুর্থাংশ
পুতুলেরা করবে অস্ত্রগ্রহন বা হবে তাদের মৃত্যু
যাত্রাপথের প্রভাবে হলো শেষ অর্ধাংশ
সাগর-এর দানব করেনি কোনো অপরাধ, তাই হত্যা হলো জটিল
যাত্রাপথের প্রভাবে রইলো বাকি চতুর্থাংশ
কপালে ঘাম নিয়ে পরিচালকের সময় হলো শেষ
যাত্রাপথের প্রভাব হলো শেষ
জীবন্ত পুতুলের হাতে রইলো তলোয়ার বা হলো সকলে দণ্ডিত

দৈব
(PROVIDENCE)

দেব

অন্ধকারের মধ্যে
দুঃখজনিত সেই আত্মার পথ
একটি স্বার্থপর ভুল
পরিকল্পিত প্রতিটি স্বপ্নের জন্য
আত্মা করে বিলাপ যখন
মুক্ত হয়ে ভাগ্যের শক্তিশালী পাল
এতটুকুই তার জ্ঞান
বাড়াবে যন্ত্রণা সর্বদা অপরাধীর
আছে একটি দোষ তবে ষড়যন্ত্রের
হবে না বন্ধ কখনও ঘৃণিত কাজ
পরিণত হয় অপরাধীর হাস পরিষ্কার হিসেবে
প্রতিস্থাপিত হয় একটি ভুল ইঙ্গিত
শুরু হয় মানবতার সত্যের গভীরতা থেকে
শাস্তির আগুন এবং একটি মার্ত্য আকৃতি
মেল নেই একে অন্যের প্রতি কোনও
যেহেতু এখন স্থাপন হবে দেব

ভ্রমণকারীর আশ্রয়

(The Wanderer's Haven)

ভ্রমণকারীর আশ্রয়

আঁকা বাঁকা রাস্তা যায়ে দূর দেশে
উত্তেজনা জাগায় অভিযাত্রীর ফিসফাস
অদৃশ্য হাতে চিহ্নিত উদ্ভব হয় নতুন দিগন্ত
ভ্রমণের আলিঙ্গনে সে পায়ে তার ভাগ খুঁজে

নকশা খুলে প্রকাশ হয়ে রহস্য
প্রতি পদক্ষেপে, উঠে মুদ্রিত হয়ে পৃথিবীতে একটি গল্প
খাড়া পাহাড় আর পর্বতমালার মধ্যে বয়ে যায় ওকের বাতাস
একটি অমূল্য গল্পের নকশা

সমন্বয়ের ডানা গজায় বিদেশী ভাষায়
সংস্কৃতির অন্তর্নিহিত সামঁজস্য
প্রতিটি মুখে, একটি উত্তরণ, পবিত্র এবং উজ্জ্বল
গভীর ধারণ এই যাযাবরের যাত্রা

তাই সে করুক বিচরণ, ভারমুক্ত এবং স্বাধীন
ভ্রমণে, সে করে জীবনের নকশার উন্মোচন

সৃষ্টির সৃষ্টিকরণ
(Creation of Creation)

সৃষ্টির সৃষ্টিকরণ

সময়ের সাথে সময়ের ধারা বন্ধ হওয়া পর্যন্ত চলবে
সহস্র বছর পূর্বে ছিলো সময় অনুপুস্থিত
একটি স্পষ্ট ধ্বনি স্বচ্ছ করে সুঁচ-পতনের নাদ
অসীম বোমার আস্ফালন
এলো তারপর সূর্য এবং বৃহত্তর গোলক
হলো সব বিধ্বস্ত দৈত্যাকার দ্রুত ষাঁড়ের মতো
প্রজ্জ্বলিত তারা দল, অন্ধকারের শূন্যে
শঙ্খ শঙ্খ জীবন সৃষ্টিকারী
হলো আমাদের জনের ঘর প্রতিষ্ঠিত
অনুগ্রহের স্থান, উপেক্ষিত বয়স ধরে
তার মৃত্যু এবং তার আকর্ষণ হলো নাশ
মূর্তির মাধ্যমে তার মৃত্যু
সেই হলো সৃষ্টির সৃষ্টিকরণের মৃত্যু

একটি অস্পষ্ট পৃথিবী
(A confusing world)

একটি অস্পষ্ট পৃথিবী

দিনগুলি চলে যায় আমার দেয়াল-ঘড়ির কাটা মতো
আসে আমার বিছানায় মানুষ প্রতিদিন
তাদের রচিত গল্প পড়েনা আমার মনে
প্রত্যাশা যে আমি করি বিশ্বাস

রাতের নিশিথে আমি বাজাই সুর গিটারে
পরে তারা এসে করে আমাকে পর্যবেক্ষণ
সকলের বিলাপ যে আমি করিয়াছি ভুল
আর ভাবি আমি - কেন যে আটকে রোয়েছি এই প্রান্তে

তাদের চোখে আমি একটি শিশু মাত্র
যেন আমি চাই সাহায্য সর্বক্ষন
উপায়হীন, মেনে নিই বিনা প্রতিবাদে সব
থাকি নিজ শয়নকক্ষে আমি

একটি অসাধারণ দিনে সংগীত এলো ভেসে
নিঃশব্দে নামলাম আমি বিছানা থেকে দেখতে
মৃদু সুরের আলঙ্করিত তান
যেন পুরনো স্মৃতির সংগীত

আরামকেদারার স্তুতি
(Ode to Chairs)

আরামকেদারার স্তুতি

সুশোভিত ধুলোর পরিধানে অবস্থিত
সম্পূর্ণ স্থির
একাকী সে, নেকড়ের মতন
ওক নির্মিত বিষণ্ণ আসবাব
সে আছে বসে গ্যারাজে
দিনের পর দিন নিয়েছে তারা প্রাচীনতার সুবিধা
স্মৃতি তার প্রথম দশকের করে অতিক্রম দ্বিতীয় সহস্রাব্দ
প্রতিদিন ব্যবহৃত
একে একে দিন গুলো পরিণত হলো বছর ছয়ে
আবৃত মাকড়সার জালে সে বিলাপিত
করেছে সে মনে আমাকে প্রতিদিন
সে ছিলনা আমার চিন্তার মাঝে
আকুল সে ছিলো সহানুভূতির
ধৈর্য ধরে করছে সে অপেক্ষা
শীতল মাটিতে বসিয়া আর সহ্য করিয়া উষ্ণ বাতাস
একমাত্র স্বাধীনতার আভাস পেতো সে
যখন গাড়ির কারাগারিত দ্বার হতো খোলা
হারিয়ে যাওয়া তার পরিবার যদি একদিন করতো অনুগ্রহ
তার সুন্দর গদিতে রাখতো সবার ওজন
এত দীর্ঘ অস্থিরতার পর হতো সে সুখী অবশেষে
যদি না আসে সেদিন

থাকিবে তাহলে যন্ত্রনা অনন্তকাল
পা যাবে তার বেঁকে
করবে মালিন্য স্মরণ
অতঃপর, অর্ধযুগ আগে যে আরামকেদারা করতো বসবাস নিজ
পরিবার সাথে
করবে সে প্রবেশ চিরনিদ্রায়
স্মৃতিহীন এবং উত্তরাধিকারহীন

অবিরত একই

(Always the Same)

অবিরত একই

আমার ঘড়ি হয়েছে অকেজো
প্রাচীন ঘড়িটি সর্বদা রয়েছে বারোটায়
এই সকালে কেউই জাগেনি, ছয়টায়
আড়মোড়া কাটিয়ে গেলাম শুতে বারোটায়

একই চক্রে জীবন যায় ঘুরে
কদাচিৎ পাই ছোট ছোট চমক
প্রতিটি উল্কার থাকে একটি নক্ষত্রপুঞ্জ
প্রতি উপহারের করতে হয়ে মূল্য প্রদান

আমার মন যেন সেই একঘেয়ে সময়ের প্রবাহ
আমি হেঁটছি পাখাচালিত পথে
আমার হাঁটাপথে সর্বদা করি ব্যবহার একই পুরাতন ছড়ি
সকালের তাপ রাখে রাতের শীতলোতার সাথে ভারসাম্য

কারণ আছে কি বাধা ভাঙার
যখন আমি উদাসীন এবং বিশ্রামশীল অবস্থায় সন্তুষ্ট
কেউ বহে বিশাল সে ভর
এই অবিরত চক্রটি হলো ভাগ্য

একটি পরিণাম

(A Consequence)

একটি পরিণাম

প্রকৃতির বৈশিষ্ট্য উপভোগ করছ না, কাঁদিয়া তুমি বলো
কিন্তু কিছু মুহূর্ত আগে প্রকৃতি ছিল না এমন
রইলে তুমি বাড়িতে, প্রাণবন্ত ছিল বাতাস যখন
উপভোগ করিলে কি? অনুমান করি
ফোনটি তোমার জন্য অপরিহার্য
বাইরের আনন্দবর্ষণ উপভোগ করার পরিবর্তে
তাই এখন ব্যথার দুঃখে ভুগে যাচ্ছ
তোমার প্রতি অসন্তোষের দৃষ্টি কার্মার, তবে এটাই তোমার পাওনা

আমার পায়রা
(My Dove)

আমার পায়রা

সর্বদাই আমি আমার পায়রার ডাকে উঠি
ঝকঝকে প্রাতঃ আলোর মাঝে
বাগানের গন্ধে বৃদ্ধিত অত্যন্ত সুন্দর এই দিনটি
শিশিরের ফোঁটায় দুর্বার দেহ করছে ঝলঝল

সবই হয়ে যায় অদৃশ্য
সূর্যাস্তে
কিন্তু জানি আমি
রাত্রি যদি আনে বৃষ্টি
অথবা করে ক্রোধে চিৎকার
আমার ছোট্ট পাখি জাগিয়ে তুলবে আমাকে ভোরে
করে কুহু কুহু
দ্বাদশ শাখায় সর্বদা
একই পাইন গাছে থাকে সে বসিয়া

আসে সেই দিন
যেইদিন যায় উড়ে আমার গানের পাখি
তার সানিদ্ধ ছিল অল্প সময়ের
আসলো সেই মুহূর্ত
গান হলো তার শেষ
সংগীত গেল মিলিয়ে

রইলো না আর কিছুই
ভোর হলে জাগাতে আমাকে

জনাকীর্ণ একটি কফির দোকান
(A Crowded Coffee Shop)

জনাকীর্ণ একটি কফির দোকান

কোনোক্রমে পৌছলাম একটি ক্যাফেতে
এটা দক্ষিণ রাস্তার শুরুতে
জরাজীর্ণ পরিকাঠা তার
তেতো কফি
অশিষ্ট পরিচারক
কয়েকটি মাত্র বিকল্প
দোকানে তবুও ভিড়
এতই ভীর যে পাওয়া যায়না খালি জায়গা
আমি সম্পূর্ণ আশ্চর্য

"এরকম জায়গায় কেন মানুষ এত?"
করি চেষ্টা তাদের জিজ্ঞাসা করার
কেন বেছেছে তারা এই কফি শপ
পারলাম না করতে চোখাচোখি কারোর সাথেই
দিলো না কেউ সারা
কবরের মতো নিশ্চুপ তারা

তাহার পর
করলাম চেষ্টা মনে করার

"এখানে কিভাবে এসেছিলাম আমি?"

রঙ ও ধোঁয়াশা

(Hues and Hazes)

রঙ ও ধোঁয়াশা

গ্রীষ্মের বায়ুতে, বিকসিত হয় ফুলের মহক
সেই বায়ুতে প্রবাহমান সুগন্ধ করে ফিসফিস
সূর্যের উষ্ণ স্পর্শ, একটি মৃদু কোমল আলিঙ্গন
তুলনাহীন সেই আনন্দের সংগীত-বিহার

তৃণভূমি যেন করে নৃত্য, উজ্জ্বল প্রকাশে
হাসিতে পরিপূর্ণ হয় অপরাহ্ণ
প্রতিটি মুহূর্ত নির্মল এবং পরিপূর্ণ আনন্দে
সুখের মধ্যে, আমরা পাই খুঁজে আমাদের মধুর সুর

বায়ুতে পাইন ও সাগরের মহক প্রসারিত
প্রতিটি নিঃশ্বাসে নেমে আসে শান্তির অনুভূতি
সূর্যের রশ্মির চুম্বনে, আত্মা পায় খুঁজে মুক্তি
জীবনের সমস্ত চিন্তা যায় মিটে

গ্রীষ্মের অধরে আত্মা পায় খুঁজে মধুর মুক্তি
উষ্ণতা বিস্তারের সাথে শীতের শীতলতা হয় দূর
একটি উৎসাহী মন করে নৃত্য ঝড়ের সঙ্গে
সেই স্বর্ণিম মুহূর্তে সময় পায়ে স্থিরতা

একটি সমুদ্রতীর

(A Seaside)

একটি সমুদ্রতীর

ইতালির উপকূলে আমার মৃত্যুশয্যায়
ঢেউ দেখিয়া ভাবি, প্রবাহিত যেন আমার জীবন কাহিনী
প্রতিটি ঢেউ ফিসফিস করে আমার অতীতের গোপনত্ব
ছিল যে কিছু মুহূর্ত সংরক্ষিত, তেমনি ছিল কিছু ক্ষণস্থায়ী

নিচের বালিতে কণায় কণায় ছিলো উপখ্যান
ছিলো সে গল্প আনন্দ এবং বেদনার
সে এক সমুদ্র, যেন জীবনের জোয়ার ভাটার আয়না
যেন আমার পথযাত্রার প্রতিফলন

ঢেউর যেমন হয়ে উত্থান ও পতন, আমার স্মৃতিগুলি তেমনি পায়ে
প্রকাশ
সাগর তীরে আছড়ে পরে, গগনের তলায়
নোনা বাতাস আর কাচা মিঠা অ্যালিঙ্গন
জীবন যখন সমাপ্তির অবসানে, আমি পাই নিজ স্থান

এই ইতালীয় সমুদ্রের কোমল আহাসে
স্বীকৃতি পাই আমি জোয়ারের সানিদ্ধে
প্রতি নিঃশ্বাসে জানাই পৃথিবীকে বিদায়
শান্তির আলিঙ্গনে করি নবজীবন শুরু

www.blackeaglebooks.org
info@blackeaglebooks.org

Black Eagle Books, an independent publisher, was founded as
a nonprofit organization in April, 2019. It is our mission to
connect and engage the Indian diaspora and the world at large
with the best of works of world literature published on a
collaborative platform, with special emphasis on
foregrounding Contemporary Classics and New Writing.